ence K
Life Cycle

Cows

Aaron Carr

LET'S READ
AV2
BY WEIGL™
ADDED VALUE • AUDIO VISUAL

www.av2books.com

LET'S READ AV2 BY WEIGL™
ADDED VALUE · AUDIO VISUAL

Go to **www.av2books.com**, and enter this book's unique code.

BOOK CODE

U245737

AV² by Weigl brings you media enhanced books that support active learning.

AV² provides enriched content that supplements and complements this book. Weigl's AV² books strive to create inspired learning and engage young minds in a total learning experience.

Your AV² Media Enhanced books come alive with...

Audio
Listen to sections of the book read aloud.

Video
Watch informative video clips.

Embedded Weblinks
Gain additional information for research.

Try This!
Complete activities and hands-on experiments.

Key Words
Study vocabulary, and complete a matching word activity.

Quizzes
Test your knowledge.

Slide Show
View images and captions, and prepare a presentation.

... and much, much more!

Published by AV² by Weigl
350 5th Avenue, 59th Floor New York, NY 10118
Website: www.av2books.com   www.weigl.com

Library of Congress Control Number: 2013934642
ISBN 978-1-62127-683-8 (hardcover)
ISBN 978-1-62127-684-5 (softcover)

Printed in the United States of America in North Mankato, Minnesota
1 2 3 4 5 6 7 8 9 0 17 16 15 14 13

032013
WEP300113

Senior Editor: Aaron Carr
Art Director: Terry Paulhus

Weigl acknowledges Getty Images as the primary image supplier for this title.

SCIENCE KIDS
Life Cycles
Cows

CONTENTS

All animals begin life, grow, and make more animals. This is a life cycle.

Cows are mammals. Mammals are warm-blooded animals. These animals make their own body heat.

Cows give birth to live babies. The babies can weigh up to 100 pounds. They can walk just a few hours after birth.

A baby cow drinks milk from its mother.

Baby cows are called calves.
Calves often live together
away from older cows.

11

Calves drink milk for the first six to eight weeks of life. They start eating grass after about two months.

After two months, cows are big enough to live with the rest of the cow herd.

Calves grow very quickly. They can weigh up to 400 pounds after six months.

Cows are full-grown by about four years of age. They can weigh up to 2,400 pounds.

Cows can have babies by two years of age. They carry their babies for nine months.

Cows give birth to one or two calves at a time.

Every cow has its own traits. These can be size, color, or kind of fur. Cows pass on their traits to their calves. This is why calves look like their parents.

Life Cycles Quiz

Test your knowledge of cow life cycles by taking this quiz. Look at these pictures. Which stage of the life cycle do you see in each picture?

KEY WORDS

Research has shown that as much as 65 percent of all written material published in English is made up of 300 words. These 300 words cannot be taught using pictures or learned by sounding them out. They must be recognized by sight. This book contains 56 common sight words to help young readers improve their reading fluency and comprehension. This book also teaches young readers several important content words, such as proper nouns. These words are paired with pictures to aid in learning and improve understanding.

Page	Sight Words First Appearance
5	a, all, and, animals, grow, is, life, make, more, this
6	are, own, their, these
9	after, can, few, from, give, its, just, live, mother, the, they, to, up
10	away, often, together
12	about, big, enough, first, for, of, two, with
14	very
16	by
17	four, years
18	at, carry, have, one, or, time
20	be, every, has, kind, like, look, on, why

Page	Content Words First Appearance
5	life cycle
6	cows, heat, mammals
9	babies, birth, hours, milk, pounds
10	calves
12	grass, herd, months, weeks
18	age
20	color, fur, parents, size, traits

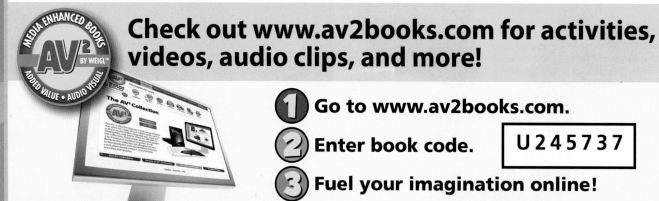